Festivals +
Celebrations

Jake's Cake

A humorous story
in a familiar setting

First published in 2006 by
Franklin Watts
338 Euston Road
London
NW1 3BH

Franklin Watts Australia
Hachette Children's Books
Level 17/207 Kent Street
Sydney
NSW 2000

A CIP catalogue record for this book is available
from the British Library.

ISBN 0 7496 6548 3 (hbk)
ISBN 0 7496 6555 6 (pbk)

Series Editor: Jackie Hamley
Series Advisors: Dr Barrie Wade, Dr Hilary Minns
Design: Peter Scoulding

Printed in China

Jake's Cake

Written by
Joan Stimson

Illustrated by
Charlotte Hard

W
FRANKLIN WATTS
LONDON•SYDNEY

Joan Stimson

"I'm better at eating cakes than making them. Luckily I have good friends who make loads of cakes for me!"

Charlotte Hard

"I love drawing. But the trouble with drawing cakes is that it makes me feel hungry!"

It was the night before
Jake's birthday.

He was having a party
and he was very excited.

Mum and Dad were downstairs in
the kitchen. They were very busy.

It was late and they still had
a birthday cake to make.

Jake crept downstairs ...

... he peered round the kitchen door.

"Can I help make my cake
for the party?" he asked.

Dad looked up from his bowl.

"No thanks, Jake," he said.

"It's time you went to sleep."

"Don't look, Jake," said Mum.

"We want your cake to be a surprise."

11

Jake went back to bed.

But he kept calling downstairs.

"Is my cake big enough?" he cried.

"Are you sure my football
friends will like it?"
"Shhh!" said Mum, "you'll
wake up your sister."

At last, Jake went to sleep, but his dreams were full of cake. Early next morning, he was wide awake.

15

Jake crept downstairs and into the kitchen. On the kitchen table was a tin.

"This must be my cake," he thought,
and he lifted the lid ...

17

"A TEDDY BEAR!" cried Jake.

"This cake is for a baby!"

Jake quickly banged the lid

back on the tin.

Then he stomped around the kitchen.

"What will my friends say?"

he groaned.

Mum, Dad and Jake's little sister,
Jess, all came into the kitchen.
"Happy birthday, Jake!" they said.

Jake said nothing. He couldn't tell them that he had looked at his cake.

Later that day, everything was ready
for the party.

Jake's friends arrived and started having fun. But Jake was not happy.

Mum and Dad disappeared into the kitchen. "Oh, no!" thought Jake.

"They're going to bring in that cake.
And all my friends will laugh."

When Dad carried in the tray,
Jake closed his eyes. But his
friends didn't laugh.

They all sang "Happy Birthday!" as
loud as they could. Jake opened his
eyes and smiled.

Dad put the tray on the table.

"It's a special footballer's cake,"

he said proudly.

"And we made a different cake
for Jess," said Mum.

"Thank you, it's brilliant!" laughed
Jake as he blew out the candles.

30

And when his friends went home,
they all took an extra slice of cake
with them.

Notes for parents and teachers

READING CORNER has been structured to provide maximum support for new readers. The stories may be used by adults for sharing with young children. Primarily, however, the stories are designed for newly independent readers, whether they are reading these books in bed at night, or in the reading corner at school or in the library.

Starting to read alone can be a daunting prospect. READING CORNER helps by providing visual support and repeating words and phrases, while making reading enjoyable. These books will develop confidence in the new reader, and encourage a love of reading that will last a lifetime!

If you are reading this book with a child, here are a few tips:

1. Make reading fun! Choose a time to read when you and the child are relaxed and have time to share the story.

2. Encourage children to reread the story, and to retell the story in their own words, using the illustrations to remind them what has happened.

3. Give praise! Remember that small mistakes need not always be corrected.

READING CORNER covers three grades of early reading ability, with three levels at each grade. Each level has a certain number of words per story, indicated by the number of bars on the spine of the book, to allow you to choose the right book for a young reader:

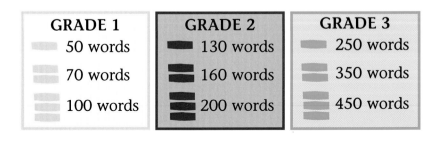

GRADE 1	GRADE 2	GRADE 3
50 words	130 words	250 words
70 words	160 words	350 words
100 words	200 words	450 words